TRAPPED WITH HER ALIEN MATE

HOLIDAY STARR

KATE RUDOLPH

STARR HUNTRESS

PUBLISHED BY KATE RUDOLPH

Last minute holiday shopping should be a breeze...

That's Jody's thought as she walks into the store. Then she spots the hottest alien she's ever seen.

But any fantasy she might have is interrupted when the next guy walks in.

He looks like Santa.

Evil Santa.

And he's got evil toys to keep her and the other shoppers locked in the store so he can do evil things to them.

Jody's determined to get out, and hot alien, Aldyn, is determined to help her.

And if they can defeat Evil Santa, she might just find a hot Detyen male in her life and under her tree.

[1]

JODY

I did this every year.

I left Christmas shopping to the last minute. I know it's a bad habit. And I'm sure if my parents were still around, they'd say something about it. Of course, they haven't been around since I was about three years old. And none of my foster parents were big on Christmas. So no one was going to call me out.

Today I needed to get gifts for my fellow teachers at school and a couple decorations for the classroom. In and out of the store in ten minutes. I could do it. And if I was lucky, I wouldn't even need to listen to the holiday songs I hated.

I wasn't going to get distracted.

Oh! Shiny.

Okay, I did *not* need a unicorn covered in sparkles and lit up with glowing lights. I really didn't. And it wasn't my style.

But it was *so* shiny.

Discipline.

I had to teach it to my preschoolers. And the best way to do that was to lead by example.

But it was so shiny.

I tore my gaze away from the unicorn and looked into the store. It was huge. One of those big box stores that carried a little bit of everything under the sun. Did I need camping equipment? Lawn furniture? Cooking supplies? Groceries? I could find it here. But what I really wanted was gifts.

The store seemed strangely deserted. Then again, it was kind of late and they were probably going to be closing soon. I should have looked at the sign on the door, but they would kick me out when they had to.

It was so deserted that I thought I was alone for a while. And then I spotted Santa and his elf sitting on a little bench at the center of the store and I couldn't help but smile.

He wasn't really Santa. I didn't believe in Santa;

well, I don't think I ever believed in Santa. Right now I was just looking at a man in a red suit and a woman in green tights with curly shoes.

But at least I wasn't alone. I wandered down an aisle, but kept glancing back at the door, wondering if someone else would enter the building. It felt a little creepy when it was this deserted. My eyes strayed over the various gift displays, but when I heard the tinkling bells over the door, something jauntily holiday-themed, almost a song I recognized but not quite, I looked over and had to bite my tongue for making a noise.

Damn.

He was an alien. A lot of them had started moving to town over the last few years. Ever since those Detyen warriors showed up and protected us from a violent alien who tried to destroy our planet. Earth had gotten quite... intergalactic all of a sudden. It was cool.

But the alien at the door didn't make me think of warriors. He made me think of bed.

No. I wasn't doing that anymore. *That* was a long time ago. Anonymous nights between the sheets were a thing of the past, and I wasn't going to break my own rules.

It took more effort than it should have to tear my eyes away from his glistening golden skin. He even looked good under fluorescent lights. How was that possible? He was wearing a bulky coat, but his pants were tight enough that I got a view of his ass that left little to the imagination. My fingers itched to touch.

Instead, I jammed them into my pocket and forced myself to turn away. My resolve lasted for all of thirteen seconds, I counted. But when I looked back he was gone. Clearly he hadn't seen me.

Or, he hadn't been interested in a mousy preschool teacher. Not that he knew I was a preschool teacher. But the mousy thing came through. I couldn't help it.

Christmas gifts, I reminded myself. In and out. Just find something.

I had made it to the end of the aisle and turned so I was almost completely out of view of the door when the bells chimed again. I tilted my head at just the right angle and spotted another Santa.

Or was he?

No, he was an alien. A shiver ran up my spine and I tried to ignore the immediate hit of revulsion. I didn't know anything about him. It wasn't cool to make judgments. But there was something about his face that I didn't like. It looked evil. He looked like an Evil Santa Claus.

He was wearing a huge red robe, and what I had first thought was a Santa hat was actually some kind of horn coming out of his head. He had a giant white beard, but it was kind of scraggly, and the hair was so thick that I wasn't sure that it was actually hair. Alien hair.

I ducked behind a giant display as he walked past. I was more than a few meters away, so there was no way he saw me, but my heart stuttered and my palms sweated.

I didn't want him to see me.

Was it because he wasn't hot? Was I that shallow? I see one alien with glistening golden skin and I want to wrap my arms around him and tug him to my bed. Another alien that's not quite as... well-built... and I'm hiding like a monster's after me.

Not good.

Then I looked even closer, careful to stay hidden. Were those tusks?

He passed between two more aisles and I got half a glimpse of them. Yeah. Tusks.

There was nothing wrong with tusks. Some aliens had them. Just because humans were tuskless didn't mean that it was automatically a bad thing.

But I wasn't about to walk out into the middle of the store so he could see me. Something told me that was a bad idea.

I just had to find the gifts and get out of there. It would be fine.

Or maybe I needed to just get out.

I walked blindly into the next aisle. It was mostly children's toys. Cars and space shuttles and little blasters. Not the actual weapons, of course. Some of my kids would love this, but I couldn't afford to get gifts for all of them. They would be happy with the candies I brought in on the last day before break.

Maybe I'd shape them like stars. They would like that.

I was ready to give up on that aisle when a woman's scream cut through the store.

I froze, unsure of what to do. What was going on? Was it Evil Alien Santa? Or maybe the other Santa? Or the hot alien? What was going on?

A braver person would have run towards the action to figure it out. Or maybe would have called the authorities. I was frozen, unable to do anything but clutch the toy I was holding like it was a real blaster.

I didn't know what to do.

The woman screamed again.

I had to move. I had to do *something*. But before I could take a step, a force hit me hard enough to knock the wind out of me and I fell to the ground as blackness swallowed me whole.

What was going on? Where was I?

My eyes flickered open and any hope that I had collapsed from low blood sugar evaporated. There was something metallic overhead and lights flashed. My body felt weird. Like I wasn't where I was supposed to be.

Was I on a spaceship?

I had never left the planet before. I didn't know what it felt like to be subject to anti-grav. But a quick shift of my head revealed the toys that I had been looking at only a few minutes ago.

Was it a few minutes? How long had I been out?

Why had I been out? I had never fainted before in my life. I hadn't been feeling sick. Had the Evil Santa done something?

I had no proof. No reason to really think it, other than the fact that he looked kind of scary. But the suspicion made me bite back a groan as I turned over and scrambled onto my hands and knees. I didn't want to stand all the way up. With the way my stomach was roiling and my vision was fuzzy, I wasn't sure that I could. And I wasn't going to risk falling back over and making a noise.

I had to stay quiet.

Something was up. I had to figure out what, or there was no getting out of the situation. Or maybe I had hit my head when I fell, and now I was suffering from paranoid delusions.

Wouldn't I know if I was suffering from paranoid delusions?

No. That's why they call them delusions.

I was getting sidetracked. Delusions or not, I needed to act, otherwise I was never getting out of the aisle.

Crawling wasn't as easy as some of my preschoolers made it look. The floor underneath me was some kind of hard tile, and though it looked clean when I was standing up, now that I had my hands on it I could tell it was filthy.

I shuddered. Gross.

I kept my head down. Eventually I made it to the

edge of the aisle, where I could peek out and see what was going on. Was I the only one who had collapsed? Was this really something that was just about me? Or had the other people in the store been affected?

My answer came swiftly.

It wasn't just me. The human Santa and his green-clad elf were sitting against a counter and they looked terrified. From the vicious look on Evil Santa's face, it was obvious why. He had done something. He was saying something. Ranting. But I was too far away to make it out. I didn't even know if he was speaking English.

I didn't have a subdermal translator. They were expensive, and I didn't really need one in my day-to-day life. So hopefully the alien either had a translator of his own or he spoke English. And maybe he just looked angry. Hopefully.

Resting alien bitch face. It was a thing. Right?

Given the way human Santa and the elf flinched away from his latest roar, it wasn't resting alien bitch face.

Damn. I crawled back into the aisle before anyone could see me. But not before I saw Evil Santa banging something against the counter. It was dark and small enough to be held in his hand. A communicator? No way to know without getting close. And there was no way I was getting close.

But that made me think of my own communicator. If something was up... if he was doing something to us... if he wanted to hold us hostage... I needed to get help here.

I pulled my communicator out of my pocket and pressed the screen to wake it up. Nothing happened. I pressed again and still nothing. And then I pressed the power button, hoping that maybe it had just accidentally turned off.

Still nothing.

Completely blank screen.

What the hell? I knew it had been completely charged when I'd walked into the store. It was important to me that I never ran out of battery. I hated the idea of being stranded somewhere with a useless communicator.

So why was it dead? It wasn't exactly the most high end device on the market, but it had served me well for the past couple of years. It had never died on me before.

Could it be something that Evil Santa was doing? He possibly had the power to knock people unconscious without being near them. Could the same go for communicators?

Bad thought. I did *not* like the sound of that. And I didn't want to stick around for much longer.

It felt risky to go for the entrance of the store. But I was pretty sure Evil Santa couldn't see the doorway from where he was standing. Besides, he was faced away from the door and yelling at the other humans. Even better, the doors remained all the way open. He wouldn't even hear the whispering slide as it opened and closed. It was just a doorway. If I could get there I could get out and get help.

It was risky. Really, really risky. He didn't know I was back here. I could just stay curled up in a corner, maybe find a display to hide myself behind, and hope that he went away before things got even worse.

That would save me. Maybe. Only if Evil Santa didn't start looking around for other people. He would have to eventually. The store was too big to assume that only human Santa and his elf were there.

What about that other alien?

I didn't know where he had gone. And I hadn't seen him when I'd spotted Evil Santa. Were they working together?

I had no reason to think that. Just because they were aliens didn't mean they were friends.

So could I find that alien? Could he help me? Could he hide with me?

I was a coward. There were at least two people being held hostage. I thought they were being held hostage. And here I was thinking of staying hidden and letting whatever happened to them happen.

Not good. I couldn't do that to them. I had to get help. I was in the position to do it.

That meant I had to get out the front door. Surely there were other exits in the building. There had to be a back way in for deliveries and maybe an employee entrance. But I was backed into a corner. There were only a few aisles where I was crawling, and if I wanted to get to the rest of the store I would need to go into that central area where Evil Santa was standing.

My only option of escape was the front door.

I had to try it.

I crawled even slower than I had earlier. If this was my one chance of escape I couldn't screw it up. I didn't want Evil Santa to see me. But I also didn't want human Santa or the elf to see me either. I didn't think they would sell me out. They looked terrified. But they might accidentally give me away.

I made it to the edge of the aisle and had to stop. This was where it got dangerous. There were a few displays between me and the entrance. I could use them for cover. Could put them between myself and Evil Alien Santa. I had to hope it was enough.

I wanted to move fast. Wanted to get up and sprint for the door. But speed like that would draw attention to me. Attention I could not afford.

So I moved slowly. Achingly slowly. So slow that I could practically feel the blood pounding in my veins. Every beat of my pulse sounded like a banging drum. But I made it to the door. I could almost feel the cold wind from outside blow on me.

Why couldn't I feel it? I should be able to feel it.

I crawled towards the opening, but before I could cross the threshold, my body met some sort of resistance. It wasn't a door. There was no door there.

It was a force field of some kind. I tried again, throwing myself at the opening. But nothing happened. It didn't hurt, but I couldn't go through.

This was bad. Very, very bad. I was exposed, and if Evil Alien Santa looked my way he would see me. I scrambled back towards the aisle. Something was keeping the door shut. Or rather, keeping a force field in front of the door. That was very, *very* bad.

And I had a feeling it had something to do with the device in Evil Alien Santa's hand. Or maybe he had another device. Maybe the device in his hand served an even more nefarious purpose. One that clearly wasn't working.

Apparently the frustration a person felt at a malfunctioning remote-shaped device was the same no matter the species.

"Puny human, are you crying? Are you scared?" The sound of his voice was enough to make my stomach turn. He sounded like he was a minute away from torturing puppies.

"My name is Jeff." That had to be human Santa. Jeff. And Jeff sounded scared, his voice trembling. I wanted to help him, but I was frozen in place. "And she's Wendy," he continued, some of his fear transforming to bravado. "We're not puny. What are you doing? Let us go."

Evil Santa let out a little laugh. It sent a shiver of terror down my spine. "You will be tribute for my brother. He will have a feast unlike any he's ever known. I will bring honor to my family." He got loud at that declaration, almost loud enough to make my ears hurt.

"You're going to eat us?" Wendy asked.

I was glad she did. Because *tribute* and *feast* were not words I wanted to hear from an evil-looking alien who was holding us all hostage.

Evil Alien Santa did not respond. Wonderful. My

wrists and knees were starting to ache. I didn't know how long I'd been crawling around. It felt like hours. It had probably been two minutes.

I had just come here to buy Christmas presents. How did I end up getting held hostage by Evil Alien Santa?

What was I going to do? He was just one man. He didn't seem to have any sort of special powers. Except for the whole knocking us all out thing. But I didn't know if that was a psychic power or if he had used a tool of some kind.

If I turned myself in, maybe I could help Jeff and Wendy and we could overpower Evil Alien Santa together. The eight foot tall alien with tusks and a giant horn coming out of his head.

Yeah. That wasn't going to work.

But how was he going to get us to his brother? It sounded like he wanted to abduct us. Was a space-ship coming? A shuttle of some kind? Or maybe he wanted to teleport us.

That wasn't good. None of this was good. But if he was using a teleporter, we would disappear before anyone had any idea we were even in trouble. A shuttle at least might call some attention to the place.

I still didn't know what to do. I couldn't think.

Tears pricked at the corners of my eyes, and I was afraid that I was going to start crying at any minute. I wasn't a pretty crier. There was snot and gasping and a whole host of other things that really just didn't look great. Worst of all, I would definitely call attention to myself. I did not want to do that. I had to stay hidden.

I had to get help. Somehow.

I was trying to think. Trying to figure something out. But before I could do anything a hand collapsed around my mouth, making me swallow my gasp of terror and pulling me deep into the aisle.

[3]
ALDYN

Denya.

I didn't get a good enough look at her when I first walked into the store, but once I got close, the recognition tore through me.

My mate.

The one person in all of the worlds, all of the galaxies, who could save my life. Of course, that life hadn't been in such immediate danger until a few moments ago. I didn't know what sort of tool the alien who had us trapped was using, but I didn't like it. I had seen a lot of things in my twenty-eight years but never this.

Not exactly.

Force field? Sure. Teleporters? Of course. But some kind of tool that could knock people unconscious from a distance? No. That was something different altogether. And I didn't like it. There was no use giving him the benefit of the doubt. This guy wanted to hurt us.

But he hadn't yet caught my denya.

No, she was in my arms. Quivering. Quaking. She was scared, and it was all my fault.

Shame washed through me. But if I let her go I was afraid she was going to scream and give us both away before we could find a way out of the store. And I would be lying if I said I didn't enjoy the feel of her body pressed against mine.

I had to find out her name. Was it so much to ask? She was beautiful. Human. With deep brown eyes and dark hair hidden by a cap. I couldn't help myself as my free hand reached up and removed it, freeing the silken strands. They wove around my fingers as if they had a life of their own.

I wanted her laid out on my bed.

But I couldn't think of that now. Not when we were in such danger. Not when the alien holding us captive could find us at any moment. Would she scream if I let her go? Was she going to help me get out of this mess?

She was my mate. I trusted that she was capable. No mate of mine would give up so easily. It took a certain inner strength to be mated to a Detyen. We had problems of our own.

Most of those problems were solved by the mating. But she didn't know about that yet. She was human.

It was a miracle that humans could be our mates. My species, the Detyens, had only found that out in the last few years. But it was why so many of my people had flocked to Earth.

In the two years since I had moved here I hadn't even gotten a hint of recognition. I had begun to give up hope.

Despite the dire situation, hope was all I could feel now.

But she had to work with me first. We had to figure a way out of here. I didn't want us to become victims of the alien that was holding us captive.

I wanted to know her name.

"Don't scream."

[4]
JODY

His hand was warm. Why was I focusing on that?

We fell back into the aisle and I was terrified that Evil Santa would hear. We lay there for several seconds, breathing heavily. The alien behind me was like a furnace. At some other time I might've wanted to burrow into him. To feel his skin against mine. But not today.

Not now.

"Keep it down," he said, his lips close enough to brush against my ear and make me shiver. "We don't want him to catch us."

No, no we did not. I was happy to know that this alien was on my side. Or at least he wasn't on the side of Evil Santa. I was willing to call that a win. For now.

He let go of me, removing his hand from my mouth and putting just a bit of space between us. I turned around and got a good look at him.

The glimpse I'd gotten earlier when I walked into the store didn't do him justice. His skin glowed golden, and though he was wearing a winter coat, I caught sight of dark markings peeking out around his neck. His eyes were dark, his lips full.

God, what would they taste like?

Not now, brain. It wasn't the time. It would *never* be the time. We were in the middle of a crisis and I didn't know this guy. And I didn't sleep with guys I didn't know.

Not anymore.

I didn't like to think about that time in my life. It had been a few years since I'd ended most of my nights in strangers' beds. I was doing better now. Starting to respect myself more. I was determined to actually *feel* something for a person that I invited that close to me.

Or to at least know their last name.

And sometimes their first name.

But I didn't want to think about former self-destructive tendencies or an extra-long dry spell. Though to be honest, it was better to think of that than what would happen if Evil Alien Santa caught us.

It wasn't like I was going to jump into bed with this guy. Well, we didn't need a bed. And in a store this big, we could probably find one anyway. I was pretty sure those displays were near the back.

No. I had to behave. I needed discipline. We were in a crisis. Why was I so distracted?

Probably because it was better to think about a hot guy than the alien trying to hold us hostage and turn us into *tribute*.

"Who are you ?" I asked. "What's your story?" Christmas music played loud enough to cover the sound of our talking, but I still whispered. Who knew if Evil Santa had super hearing? I wasn't looking forward to finding out.

He whispered right back. He was still close, but no longer holding onto me. I missed it. "I'm Aldyn. Detyen, since I can see you're wondering. Can't say I'm too happy to be held hostage by that guy." He grimaced and glanced down the aisle as if he was checking to see that Evil Santa was keeping his distance.

Detyen. Yeah that's what I thought. I remembered researching them when they showed up on Earth a while back. There was *something* about them.

Something *weird*. It had made me sad. But I couldn't remember right now. And unless he had a hidden power, it probably didn't matter. "I'm Jody. Human. Do you have laser eyes?"

Aldyn looked at me like I'd grown a second head. No. There were aliens with two heads. He was looking at me like I was even weirder. "No. No laser eyes," he said slowly, sounding out the words as if to make sure he was clear about what I was asking.

Great. Hot alien Aldyn was going to think I was crazy. Not exactly how I wanted to start this relationship. Not that we were in a relationship. I had to keep my mind out of the gutter.

"I heard Evil Santa say that he wanted us as tribute for his brother." I didn't know if Aldyn had heard that, and it seemed like a good piece of information to share. "Not quite sure what that means. But it doesn't sound good."

I could have sworn that Aldyn's eyes turned red for a second, but it must have been a trick of the light. In no time they were back to black. "No," he agreed. "It does not sound good. Evil Santa?" He grinned.

And despite the situation, his grin was infectious. My heart was light as I smiled back, even if only for a moment. "Do you know about Santa?"

There was no telling how long he had been on the planet and if he knew our traditions or not. But he nodded. "Well. He looks like Evil Santa. I don't think real Santa would actually kidnap people or hold us hostage."

Aldyn clamped a hand over his mouth as if it was the only thing keeping him from laughing.

Something warm bubbled up within me. Now was *not* the time for flirting. But I liked that I could make him laugh. Maybe when this thing was over... Yeah, we had to focus on getting out first. There was no telling how long that could take. If we could even do it. "Something's blocking the door," I added. "I tried to get out, but I couldn't."

"I saw." Any of the earlier mirth had evaporated and he looked serious. "I think he's trying to open a portal to a ship so he can deliver us. It looks like the transponder is broken, which is the only thing that's keeping us on this planet for now."

"Why do you think that?" Sure, I had thought something about teleportation, but I didn't really know anything about it. It's not like it was something I encountered every day.

"That tool that he's banging against the counter." He nodded back towards the center of the store but didn't try and move. "It kind of looks like a portal transponder. Our best chance out here is to get that thing away from him. Then we can figure out what he's doing to keep us inside the building."

I had another idea. "Or we could figure out the building thing first," I suggested. "He can't exactly teleport us if he can't get his hands on us." I felt a little bad even suggesting it. Good Santa and Wendy the elf didn't exactly have a chance to escape if me and Aldyn got out. But we could go for help. We wouldn't just abandon them.

"That would also work," Aldyn agreed, but he didn't seem as enthusiastic. Maybe he secretly had heroic instincts.

He was looking at me intently. And not just in a way that acknowledged that we were the only two people who could get ourselves out of the situation. He was looking at me like he wanted to eat me. But in the good way. In the way I tried not to think about too much anymore. In the way that lit my body up and made me want to pull him close and see *exactly* what we could do before we got caught.

Such a bad idea. I wasn't going to risk our only chance of escape by getting hot for an alien and making out in a Christmas toy aisle. I had to have some standards.

But damn, did he live up to them.

If I survived this, I was going to kiss him.

Unless he had like a wife or a husband or like a dozen partners or something. But I didn't know anything about Aldyn's life other than the fact that he was hot and I needed him. That was far more than I knew about anything else going on at the moment. And I was getting tired of sitting and waiting. "So," I said. "What do we do?"

My heart was beating so hard that I was sure it was going to give us away. There was no way out. Evil Santa had us trapped, and even with Aldyn at my side I didn't see how he was going to help.

What could we do?

Try to escape, I guess. It was our only chance. We had to get out of there. Had to find help. Had to hope that Evil Santa didn't do anything to Jeff or Wendy before we got back. He wanted us in good condition for his brother, so that was something.

I guess.

I still didn't like it. But what were we supposed to do?

Our plan was to find another way out. I hadn't been willing to try it at first. The section of the store Aldyn and I were sitting in was kind of isolated. We couldn't sneak down the aisles to find a different exit. We would have to risk going out into the main part of the store where Evil Santa could see us. We would have to be quick. And we would have to hope that Jeff and Wendy didn't give us away.

Before we got up, Aldyn looked at me for a long moment. There were unspoken words written across his face. But I couldn't read them. Maybe they were in whatever alien language he spoke.

Or maybe I was just reading into the situation.

We stuck together. Splitting up would have let us cover more ground, but it felt too risky. If it came to it, the two of us might be able to fight off Evil Alien Santa. *If* he didn't have any other tricks up his sleeves. That was a big if. He'd already knocked us out with one of his toys and apparently could teleport us the second he got the transponder to work. I didn't think Aldyn and I would be a match. But we had to try.

Aldyn and I got to moving. My hands were shaking and I shoved them in my pockets. I wasn't going to accidentally knock something over because I couldn't control my body. We made it to the edge of the farthest aisle and luck was with us this time. Evil

Santa was facing Jeff and Wendy and not paying any attention to us.

"You're weak," Evil Santa told Jeff in a voice of pure evil. "An insignificant human. You can't even save the woman you love."

Wendy gasped, and even I felt the surprise. "J-Jeff?" It came out with a little stutter. I couldn't look away, even though I knew we had to keep moving. Aldyn grabbed onto my wrist and tugged me deeper into the store. I could still hear them.

"Why didn't you tell me?" she asked.

"The time never seemed right." Jeff's voice sounded pained, and I didn't know if he was hurt or if it was from the revelation.

Evil Santa made a sound of disgust. "You humans waste your time. I'm doing you a favor."

"How did you even know that?" Wendy demanded.

He grunted. "Such small minds you humans have. I can see the truths that you refuse to speak. You can hide nothing from me."

I shivered. I really *didn't* like the sound of that. Unspoken truths? I had more than a few of those. And I didn't like the fact that Evil Santa could tell who was naughty and who was nice like that.

Was his species how we got legends of Santa?

Was he just one of the evil ones? Or had Santa always been evil? I didn't have time to worry about that. We had to keep moving.

Aldyn and I had more freedom to move once we got out of that isolated section of the store. I followed behind him, conscious of every squeak of my shoes against the hard floor. Did Evil Santa hear it? Would he be coming for us? Please no.

But he must have heard something. Or somehow sensed it. Could he tell those unspoken truths if he couldn't see us?

He made a commotion and started heading our way. Aldyn tugged hard on my arm to get me to squeeze beside him in the tiniest alcove I had ever seen. It shouldn't have fit two people. And from the way we had to stand flush up against one another, it really didn't. But the shadows mostly concealed us from the rest of the store. And from the way the alcove was built, as if it were a little hiding place for the store to keep extra inventory, Evil Santa would only be able to see us if the angle was exactly right.

Aldyn's body felt *so* good.

It had to be the panic talking. It was making me react in ways I knew I shouldn't. But I couldn't help but lean even further back into him. And when he let out a choked groan, my body heated as if it were on fire.

Was that his cock?

His hand came around to press against my stomach, as if he were holding me in place. He needed to go a little higher or a bit lower to make it count. But we couldn't. Not when we were hiding from Evil Alien Santa and being held hostage in a department store.

A shadow fell across the alcove and I held my breath. A second passed. And then another. And then the shadow went away.

He was gone.

But we stayed in the alcove for another few minutes. We had to be sure he wouldn't see us when we got out. Our luck had held for this long, but I didn't think it would hold much longer. We had to find a door.

When we were satisfied that we were safe...ish, we took careful steps outside the alcove. Evil Santa was nowhere to be seen. I let out a relieved breath and somehow shifted my weight. I didn't even realize I did it. But my hip brushed against one of the displays and a large box went tumbling to the ground.

It was as loud as a bomb. And the shockwave could have sent me flying backwards.

Of course, there wasn't a real shockwave. That was just my mind knowing that I had fucked everything up. Aldyn and I started running. There was no use for stealth now. Not when Evil Santa was going to find us.

We took off in the same direction. Our feet pounded against the floor and my lungs heaved. I was no sprinter. But I found a depth of endurance I hadn't known I was capable of. Aldyn took a turn, but I kept running straight. Hopefully it meant that Evil Santa couldn't find us both. I didn't want him to find Aldyn. I wanted him to find me even less. Where was the door? I just had to find the door.

"Run all you want," Evil Santa taunted. "My portal will suck up every living thing in this store. You will be my brother's tribute whether you want it or not."

No escape. Just like we thought.

Fuck.

I couldn't run much longer. I was shaking, and I could barely breathe. I had to hide. I found another one of those alcoves and snuck in as far as I could. Maybe Evil Santa was right and his teleporter would suck me up when he got it working. But if he stopped looking for me, at least I could try and escape and go get outside help.

I hoped.

Just like before, his footsteps echoed down the aisle and his shadow passed the alcove. But this time there was no Aldyn to hold me close. I hadn't realized just how much comfort he had given me until now. The shadow walked by and I let out a breath. He hadn't seen me. I wasn't safe.

But I was safe enough.

I thought that too soon.

A hand reached into the alcove and grabbed my shirt, yanking me out.

[6]

ALDYN

Where was Jody?

I took a turn and suddenly she wasn't there with me. My heart yelled at me to double back. That was my mate back there. She needed help. But I was of no use to her if I got caught.

Our captor, Evil Santa, as Jody called him, started taunting me. I blocked him out. There was no use listening to him. I just had stay out of his grasp. Had to find a way to get help, to get us all out of here before things turned ugly.

Who was I kidding? Things were already ugly.

But they could get worse. They could *always* get worse. I took another turn, careful to stay out of the main hallway. I did not want Evil Santa to catch sight of me and add me to his group of captives.

My communicator didn't work. But there were comms embedded in the wall of the store. Maybe the hardwire would get out.

It was worth a shot.

I found one. The screen was cracked and a number pad beside it had clearly seen better days. But I wasn't here to judge its aesthetics.

The machine turned on when I pressed it and I almost let out a sound of joy. Almost. I snapped my mouth shut at the last second. I wasn't going to let a stupid mistake get in my way.

The comm screen wanted a password. I assumed it was something I could type in on the number pad. I tried a few numbers, selecting the most worn digits on the pad first. But nothing happened.

Out of desperation I punched in the zero key as many times as I could.

Success!

But it became immediately clear that whatever Evil Santa was using to make my comm malfunction, it was affecting the comm on the wall as well. There was no signal. I tried making a call anyway, but it failed to connect.

I wasn't sure what to do next. Did I go back for my denya? I couldn't leave her in Evil Santa's clutches. And I had a weapon up my sleeve, or, well not quite up my sleeve. But I had a weapon he couldn't see.

I wasn't exactly a trained fighter. And Evil Santa was big.

But there were three humans out there. We could take him if we worked together. As long as he didn't have a blaster or another weapon. Or laser eyes. I smiled at the suggestion Jody had made.

My mate was a clever woman, and I could tell there was a sense of humor there ready to unfold. I wanted to find out what she would say when we weren't hiding in fear for our lives. I wanted to find out who she would be then.

But that meant I had to find a way to get us out of here.

I was getting close to the back of the store. I was pretty sure there was an exit back there. I didn't know if the force field would have it blocked off. I didn't know if it only covered the exits or the windows or the entire building. I figured I was going to find out. What other choice did I have?

Once I got outside of the building I could find some help. Find a communicator and call the police. They could end this. They were more than equipped to deal with Evil Santa.

It was a plan. Even a decent one, some would say.

But then it all crashed and burned.

Jody cried out.

Evil Santa had her. And he was going to get me next.

JODY

I tried to fight him. I really did. But Evil Santa was strong. My legs scrambled against the hard floor and there was nothing to get purchase on. There was no way to resist.

Fuck. Fuck. Fuck. *Fuck.*

He pulled me all the way into the center of the store and dropped me roughly on the ground near Jeff and Wendy. I tried to get my breathing under control. I was freaking out. But I didn't want him to see that. I didn't want him to have that power over me. I'd dealt with calamities before—little kids are chaos monsters and I'd been working with them for years. But injured children and the scary stories they tell are a completely different matter than evil aliens.

But I had to keep calm for my school kids. I had

to hope I could get back to them. And I had to hope that I didn't give Aldyn up. Evil Santa towered over me, and this close I could see that not only did he have tusks, he had fangs too. I did not want to know just how sharp they were.

I was never telling any kid a Santa story ever again. Not when *he* was going to be the guy that came to mind.

"Are you the only one out there?" he demanded.

My lips quivered and I could barely breathe but I said, "Yes," as steadily as I could.

Evil Santa scowled. He knew I was lying. It was that power to know untold truths. Or maybe I was just terrible liar. And then he did something even worse. He grinned. And it made my blood run cold. "You're not alone. Oh no. It's better than that. You're *special.*"

I hated the way he said it. I wasn't special.

I was just an orphaned girl who finally made good. Well, a woman. But I wasn't worrying about that now. I finally got my life all figured out and had figured out what I needed to do. But that didn't make me special. It just made me a person. I wanted to hit him. But he was huge and towering over me, and hitting him would just put me in a world of hurt.

No, thank you.

I didn't ask him what he meant by calling me special. I didn't want to give him the satisfaction. But I wondered. I don't think anyone had ever called me special before. At least, they hadn't meant it if they did.

I hoped Aldyn stayed hidden. He was our only chance to get out of here. If I believed in anything I would have prayed at that moment.

Evil Santa turned back towards the aisles looking for Aldyn. There was a strange awareness just at the edge of my mind. I could have sworn it was Aldyn. But that was weird and impossible. Of course my awareness, my emotions, were heightened at the moment. I couldn't actually *sense* Aldyn. I just thought I could.

It was wishful thinking.

"My brother doesn't know how many tributes I am bringing," Evil Santa yelled out to the aisles. "I can kill her and he'll never have to know. Three tributes are just as good as four. Though *you* won't last long if I do that, now will you?"

What was he talking about? I was so caught up in that question that I barely realized he'd threatened to kill me.

But I wasn't going to worry about that right now. I couldn't stop it. And I didn't think he wanted to kill me. Or maybe I just had a really strong sense of denial. I was going to cling to that for as long as I could.

But why wouldn't Aldyn last long if I died? Was that an oblique way of threatening us both?

"Show yourself if you want your mate to keep breathing." Evil Santa's tone made it clear: the time for hiding was over.

Mate? What was he talking about? Whose mate? *Me*? Aldyn? I didn't even know the guy! I was no one's mate.

I really hoped Aldyn was smart enough to stay hidden. He wouldn't be stupid enough to reveal himself. Right? Evil Santa was either going to kill me or he wasn't. I didn't want to be leverage against anyone. *Please don't be stupid.*

He was stupid.

That awareness at the edge of my consciousness told me what was going to happen right before it did. Aldyn walked out from an aisle much further away than I would have expected. He was almost to the back of the store. He could have escaped. If the door would open. His hands were up and he moved slowly. He was staring at me, and even from all the way across the store I could feel the heat of his gaze down to my soul. It was kind of unnerving. First Evil

Santa said I was special. And then Aldyn looked at me like I really was.

I wasn't. I couldn't be. But I could *almost* believe it.

"Don't hurt her," Aldyn told Evil Santa.

"I want you all in good condition. You will be excellent tributes."

I slumped down on the ground. I did *not* like the sound of that.

[8]
ALDYN

Once I gave myself up, Evil Santa didn't seem interested in me. He shoved me down by Jody and the two other humans and then turned back to the device he was messing with. Now that I got a closer look, I was sure it was a teleport transponder.

But why wasn't it working?

I knew a few things about devices. I had spent a good deal of time on Honora Station, and anyone who lived on a space station had to learn how to fix broken technology. We had to make everything work until there was no hope left of recovery.

Now that I was close to him I had an idea of why we couldn't get through the doors. Another device sat on the counter next to him. This one was larger than what he was holding in his hand, with a fragile-looking antenna sticking out of it. That was probably what was powering the force field.

And though Evil Santa didn't seem to realize it yet, I was pretty sure it was what was preventing the portal from being opened.

It was disrupting all the signals. If he figured that out, there was no hope for us. So we had to stop him before then.

Jody was shivering. I leaned in close and put my arm around her without thinking. She burrowed into me. It was only a hint of what we could have, and I wanted more. I waited for her to ask about what our evil captor had said, about her being my mate.

She said nothing.

Part of me thought I should tell her. It was her life. And mine. She had a right to know. But it would be pretty useless to worry her with that information while we were stuck here. As soon as we were free, I promised myself I would let her know. I would explain the denya bond and everything that went with it. But not until then. She deserved to be wooed. I could do no wooing here.

"You shouldn't have given yourself up," she said, barely more than a whisper. But she didn't pull away from me.

I didn't know what to say to that. From a purely tactical perspective, she was probably right. I could do a lot less to help while I was being held hostage alongside these humans than I could if I got out of the store. But he was going to kill her. And I couldn't let that happen.

"We'll get out of this," I said with a confidence I couldn't quite make myself feel.

"You sure about that?" She looked at me with disbelief written across her face.

I wanted to kiss her. She was practically daring me to with the challenge in her eyes and the curve of her lips. It might be my only chance.

But thoughts like that would get us all killed. And we were going to make it out here.

"I'm sure we'll make it out," I said with false confidence.

"Silence!" our captor yelled back at us.

I snapped my mouth shut. There was no use in upsetting him further until we had something we could do. Some way to get out of this.

I looked over at the other two humans, Jeff and Wendy. Jeff was dressed strangely, looking sort of like our captor in a human way. He had a long red coat and a fake white beard. A red cap was clutched between his hands. The knuckles of that hand had gone white. He looked like he was in pain. But I didn't see any injury. Wendy, the woman in green with short cropped black hair under a green and white cap, had her hands on his arm, resting lightly, as if she too could sense his pain. Jeff's eyes flicked over to their captor and then back to me. I didn't know if he was trying to silently ask a question or simply keep alert.

What could we say? We needed a plan. That was all tonight was. Making plans. Throwing them away. Making new plans. Getting captured.

I was never shopping again after this.

I hugged Jody even closer. Helplessness washed over me. I had a secret hidden in my hands, a weapon none of these humans could hope to match. But I didn't know what species our captor was. I didn't know if he had a secret weapon like mine. Could he slice me to bits if I got close? Did he have a blaster?

My blood ran hot and I wanted to fight him. I wanted to defend these people and get them out of here. I wanted us all safe before we could be made into tributes for this man's brother, wherever he was. But I wasn't sure how to do it.

We needed more information.

Evil Santa gave a frustrated yell and knocked

something off the counter. He glared back at us before stalking towards one of the aisles and muttering to himself. I couldn't make out the words. He probably wanted us to stay still. He was probably going to beat anybody up who dared to get to their feet.

I didn't care. This might be our only chance to figure out what was going on and get out of here. I got to my feet.

It was time to make a move.

I wanted to hiss at Aldyn to sit back down. Was he trying to get killed? Evil Santa hadn't walked that far away. He could turn around at any second. What the fuck?

Aldyn seemed to sense what I was thinking, and he scuttled back to us after only a few seconds. Just in time too. Evil Santa came back and swiped a device off of the counter and took it with him as he went a little bit further to another aisle filled with home repair equipment.

Maybe he wanted to try and fix the device he'd been screwing with for the past few minutes? I didn't know. But I was happy he was far enough away for us to try and figure out something.

He had threatened to kill me. The realization

swept over me so quickly that I would have fallen over if I hadn't already been sitting down. My hands started to shake and I curled them into fists to try and gain some semblance of control, but when I did that my teeth started to chatter.

That motherfucker had threatened to kill me.

He was going to kill us all. Whatever this tribute thing meant, whether he was sending us to his brother for us to be killed or to be enslaved, I didn't know. I didn't want to find out. We had to get out of here before that happened. And there were four of us and one of him. It didn't matter that we were scared. We had to be strong.

Aldyn sat back down next to me and put his arm around me again. I almost hated how good it felt. It was a kind of comfort that I couldn't ever remember. Of course, I'd never been in this situation before. So maybe that was it.

But a small part of my mind was still caught on the fact that Evil Santa had said that I was Aldyn's mate.

It was on the tip of my tongue to ask Aldyn what that meant. He was right there. He had to know. But what if it was something bad? What if it was something that made me... I couldn't think about it too hard. What if it wasn't something good?

No. We had worked together to get out of here. I could ask him about it later. When we were free. We couldn't get caught up on that now. If we did, we were lost.

"Anyone got any ideas?" I asked. I had to be quiet, quiet enough that Evil Santa didn't hear me. But loud enough that Jeff, Wendy, and Aldyn could. Evil Santa could come back at any minute.

"We need to take the force field down if we're going to get out the doors," said Aldyn.

No shit. "Any ideas on how to do *that*?" I asked. There was no time for snark, and I wanted to curse at myself for the bite to my words. We had to be productive.

Aldyn kept his mouth shut.

Great.

"Four on one aren't terrible odds," said Wendy. I appreciated her ruthlessness and agreed. I didn't know what kind of weapon Evil Santa had. Clearly he had that thing that could knock us out. But I didn't know if it needed to be recharged or if he could use it whenever we got annoying. I didn't particularly want to find out. But rushing him might be our only option.

Jeff shifted where he was sitting and let out a

groan. It was mostly caught in the back of his throat, but it sounded pained.

"Are you alright?" Clearly he wasn't. But the concern just popped out. Jeff's lips had gone white from his jaw being clenched and sweat beaded on his forehead. I didn't see any blood. But that didn't mean everything was okay.

Jeff shifted again and dragged his foot a few inches to the side. He groaned even louder this time, and reached out to clench Wendy's hand in his own. "I fell wrong when he knocked us out," Jeff panted. "Think I broke my ankle."

Fuck. Okay. I couldn't get caught up with that news. It was bad. Four on one odds were suddenly three on one. Still not terrible. But we had to keep defending Jeff. Stupid broken ankle.

"Any other injuries?" I had to ask. Who knew how long it would be before Evil Santa came back. We had to know what we could before then.

Luckily Wendy and Aldyn seemed okay, and so was I. "One of us can run," I suggested. "Find a way to disrupt the force field and go for help." It might have been the safest option. The other two could distract Evil Santa.

"I'm not leaving Jeff," said Wendy.

I could have guessed that.

"I can't leave you here," said Aldyn, looking at me with scary intensity.

Yeah we were *really* going to need to talk about that mate thing.

That left me. "I guess I'll have to run fast," I said. Should I be okay with leaving Aldyn? Did it make me a bad person that I was willing to run? It wasn't like I was abandoning him. I was going to get help. Aldyn seemed to have the most knowledge of what to do, so I looked at him. "Any idea on how to get the force field down?" I looked past him, hoping that Evil Santa had not made his way back. He hadn't.

Aldyn was apprehensive. Maybe he just didn't want me to go. Or maybe there was something else. "I think that larger device, the one with the antenna that he took with him, it's what's creating the force field. If we destroy that or turn it off, the force field should come down and you can get out of the store. But..." Now it was his turn to look to see if Evil Santa was coming our way. He still wasn't. Aldyn lowered his voice and we all had to lean in close to hear what he had to say. "I think the force field device is what's causing his portal not to work. The second it comes down, the portal will open and we could get sucked into wherever his brother is. So if you get out, we might not be here when help comes."

Double fuck.

I slumped on the floor. "So running is *not* an option." I wasn't going to leave them there to get sucked up into a portal and dragged somewhere across the galaxy where help would never find them.

"We could fight," Aldyn suggested. "I think it's our best chance."

It was our only chance. But Evil Santa was huge and he had to have tricks up his sleeve. He was going to hurt people. And I felt responsible for their safety. Maybe it wasn't fair. Maybe it wasn't right. But I did. It was probably the teacher in me. "Any suggestions?" I asked.

Aldyn looked determined. "We need to get him here. Then we need to get the portal opener and the force field device. And we need to destroy them both."

"Sounds like a plan."

[10]
ALDYN

I wasn't a fighter. No one would call me a warrior. There hadn't been a need for it back home and I had never considered myself the violent type.

But of the four of us, I was the best option. Especially since I was the only one with a weapon, my retractable claws. I had to win. Or at least hold out long enough for Jody and Wendy to do what they needed to do.

I had to keep our captor distracted.

The claws that lived under my skin itched to come out, but I had to hold them in. I didn't want Evil Santa to get a look before it was too late.

We thought we were going to need to start a commotion, to do something outrageous to get him to come by us. But in the end, he came back on his own.

Then all I had to do was stand up. He didn't wait for me to say anything. It was on.

He charged at me, ready for the fight. Ready to push me back down alongside the others.

But this time I was ready, wasn't willing to back down. Now it was time to battle.

I pushed back, and he was so surprised that he fell back two steps before he remembered to fight. And unlike me, he *was* a fighter. He caught me on the shoulder with a punch that was strong enough to make my entire body ache. I bit back a groan. I wasn't going to cry out from one punch.

But it hurt.

Ouch.

Evil Santa had both the force field generator and the device that would open the portal. I had to get both of them to Jody and Wendy, or at least to get him to drop them. Then Jody and Wendy would do their best to destroy them. We each had our part to play.

Jeff was too injured to do much, so he just had to try and stay out of the way.

The portal opening device was in Evil Santa's hand.

Once he got close, I unsheathed my claws and swiped across his skin. It was thicker than I expected, kind of leathery and tough to get through. But I must've hit him just right. His fingers spasmed and opened, sending that device clattering to the ground. And before he reached for it, I was on again, punching and scraping and slicing and inflicting as much damage as I could.

I tried to keep an eye out for Wendy or Jody, to see if they had made a move to recover the device, but the second I stopped paying attention, Evil Santa was on me. He hit me hard enough that my vision went blurry for a second. And after that he had my full attention. We exchanged blows and it became clear that he didn't need a weapon. He was a weapon. His fists were stronger than I'd ever encountered and he knew how to use them. I didn't think I could win.

The second time he swung for my face, my shoulder didn't save me. He got me right in the jaw and I went down. I heard Jody cry out. I wanted her near me. Wanted her right beside me, offering me comfort. It was selfish. She didn't even know me. Didn't know that I needed her. Didn't know that we were meant to be together.

My body wanted to stay curled up in a defensive ball on the ground. I didn't want to get hurt anymore. But I need to stay strong. I needed to survive. I needed to defend Jody. If I didn't survive this, we would never see what we could be together. She was my mate, my denya, and I needed to do this for her.

With strength I didn't know I possessed, I pushed myself up. Evil Santa had turned away from me and was moving to the women. I couldn't let him have them.

"Is that all you got?" I taunted. I tasted blood with every word. But it was just a split lip. I hurt, but I wasn't injured. Not yet. Not badly.

Evil Santa turned toward me. His robe gaped open and I saw the force field device sitting precariously in one of his pockets. We needed that if we were going to get out of here.

"Come on, big boy." I wiggled my fingers, inviting him to come my way. He charged.

Something possessed me, the spirit of victory, the need to defend and win. I didn't let myself worry about what he was doing to me, about the pain, about anything like that. I just had to get that force field device.

I got up real close and managed to slide my arm into his cloak and brush my fingers against the device. I didn't get a hold of it, but it was enough to knock it out of place from where it sat in his pocket and send it crashing to the ground.

Evil Santa let out a roar. He was not happy about me doing that. Good. I didn't want him happy.

But he hit even harder, and I was doing all I could to block the blows and defend myself. I got in a few hits of my own, and one even made him grunt and stumble back. But it was clear who was winning this fight. And it wasn't me. I wished I had a weapon of some kind, something even sharper than my claws. But wishing for something in the middle of a fight like this was just going to get me dead.

He charged me again and I took a step back. My foot landed on something and I heard a crunch. The force field device. Santa didn't hear it. He kept charging until he had me flat on the ground, where I landed even more fully on the device, shattering it.

At first I thought it did nothing. At first I thought we were okay. But a breathless second later, a shock-wave punched through me and out through the rest of the store.

Something started to buzz as the force field went down. I heard Jody cry out as a large portal began to open in the middle of the room.

[11]

JODY

I winced every time I saw Evil Santa hit Aldyn. It was barbaric. Horrible. And a little hot. Not Evil Santa hitting Aldyn. But when Aldyn hit back.

Were his eyes glowing red?

I couldn't look away, but I had to. Wendy and I needed to find the devices that were the key to our freedom. Aldyn was distracting Evil Santa. It was our job to get us out of there. Jeff couldn't do much but stay on the floor and try not to groan. I felt bad for the guy. He looked kind of gray, and he clearly needed a doctor. But with the force field around the building, there was no way we could get a doctor in here. We had to stop Evil Santa.

The portal device fell first. Wendy was way faster than me and managed to scramble inside, right near the fighting aliens, and grab it. Then she ran right back to me and we took a look at it. There were a bunch of buttons and some flashing lights. No instructions. Definitely nothing in English.

"Should we smash it?" I asked.

"What if that makes things even worse?" She grimaced as she asked.

Yeah, that was a risk. One I didn't want to take. I took the device from her and stared at it for a while. No ideas came to me.

And while all that was going on, Evil Santa and Aldyn kept fighting. I heard something else fall to the ground, something small, maybe plastic.

The force field device.

But before either Wendy or I could make a move, Aldyn was being flung down.

I didn't realize what happened first. How could I have known? But then a shockwave rocked through the store, sending both me and Wendy stepping back a few feet, and then a horrible buzzing sounded. I looked down at the device in my hand and then up to just behind where Evil Santa was standing.

It started as a little pinprick of light, something that might have been an optical illusion. But after just three seconds, it was clear that whatever it was, it was real and growing. The portal.

After less than thirty seconds, it was big enough for a person to crawl through, but it wasn't a person that was coming out of there. Huge tentacles flopped out and flailed around, one wrapping itself around Evil Santa. At first he seemed confident, but as it tugged on him, his expression shifted. "What's going on? What's this?" he demanded.

"It's your portal thing!" I was afraid to press any buttons, afraid to make anything worse. And I wasn't about to hand this thing over Evil Santa. Even if he was the only one who knew how to use it.

"You fool! You shifted the settings. Who knows what you have unleashed." He might've had more to say. He might have had more insults or ideas. But the tentacle thing pulled him back through the portal, and for a moment, it disappeared.

I thought maybe we were safe. I took a breath and looked at the device. There had to be a way to turn it off. Or make it bigger. Once it got to two meters wide by two meters tall, it seemed to stop growing. That was good, at least. But I didn't know what was going to come out of it. We couldn't just leave a huge portal open in the middle of the store. It was a danger to everyone.

"Figure out how to turn it off!" Aldyn yelled as he scrambled to his feet. He looked like he was about to come my way, but then another tentacle flopped out of the portal and he let out a curse. He took off toward it, those claws in his hands out and ready to do damage.

He had protected us enough. I had to figure this out.

There weren't many options. Two big buttons and one dial. There seemed to be a few other settings on the side, but I ignored them.

Aldyn let out something like a war cry as he threw himself at the tentacle, slashing at it without any mercy. It retreated, but a second later a second one joined it, and then a third, and then a fourth. Too many for one man to fight. Even a man with claws.

I had to hit something. I punched down on one of the buttons and squeezed my eyes shut, afraid of what it would do. I didn't hear anything happen, so I had to open my eyes.

Shit.

The portal had definitely grown.

I wasn't hitting that button again.

Wendy had run up to Aldyn carrying a giant pole that she must have found somewhere. It looked like it was something used to arrange products that were too high up for a person to reach. She jabbed it in towards the tentacles and it seemed to help for a moment. Then one of the tentacles grabbed onto it and tore it out of her hands. There was only one more button.

Either it worked or I screwed us all over.

"Close it, Jody. Do it now." The tentacles were wrapped all around Aldyn, and they seemed like they were about to pull him through the portal. If they pulled him through there was no getting him back. I didn't want to think about what was happening to Evil Santa right now. Sure, he had kidnapped us and that definitely wasn't cool, but being tortured by tentacles was not a fate that anyone deserved.

Okay, well from what I'd seen on the Internet, some people did really want that fate. But this was not the time to think about that.

I pressed the button.

There wasn't a shockwave this time. Instead, it was like a gust of wind as a door slammed shut. My ears popped, and when I was brave enough to open my eyes, I looked over and saw that Aldyn was standing there with two tentacles wrapped around his arms. But those tentacles didn't go anywhere. They had been chopped off by the portal closing.

I set the device carefully on the counter. I didn't want to accidentally open up another portal. But Aldyn looked ready to drop. I rushed over to him and helped pull the tentacles off.

His face was bruised and green blood was splattered over his split lip. His? He was an alien, after all. Maybe his blood wasn't red.

"Good job," he told me with a smile, and I didn't think it was even sarcastic.

"You're the one who did all the work," I said.

"I think I need to sit down." And before he could step towards a chair, he crumpled down to the floor.

[12]

ALDYN

I could feel every bruise and scrape and cut from the fight. And it was only getting worse by the second. But the portal was closed and Jody's arms were tight around me.

For the first time that night, things were looking up.

"Don't you die," she said, warning clear in her voice. "If you die, I'm going to freaking kill you."

It hurt to smile. Everything hurt. But I forced myself up from where I had fallen on the ground. I could manage to sit. But I would appreciate some medical attention soon. At least a painkiller.

Of course, from the way Jeff was groaning, he needed way more help than I did.

"No risk of dying," I told her. Not anymore. But

that was probably a conversation for a later time. I glanced over and was surprised to see how small the tentacles looked. When they had been wrapped around me I was sure they were as big as a building. But they were tiny things.

I couldn't quite circle my hands around their girth, but it would be close. They definitely didn't look as threatening now that they were cut off from whatever body they had been attached to. And I was beyond grateful I would never see that body or determine how many tentacles it normally had.

Jody and I didn't say much. After the excitement of the night, it was hard to figure out what to say. I needed to talk to her. Needed to explain who she was to me. Needed to ask her to dinner. But for several moments, I was just basking in being alive.

Sometime later, police busted through the front door, yelling a warning with their weapons drawn. But when they saw us, they seemed very confused.

"The fight's over," Jody told them, leaning her body in front of me a little as if to act as a shield. "The guy who held us captive got sucked in through a portal."

She pointed to the tentacles on the ground. "That came out of it, if you want to bag that for evidence. The portal opening mechanism is on the counter." Then she quickly added, "Don't press the button. I don't know if the portal will open back up."

The last thing we needed was to deal with that portal reopening. I much preferred Earth to whatever world we had caught a glimpse of.

The police had questions for all of us and we answered them quickly. It became clear they weren't interested in pinning the blame on anyone who'd been held hostage, and pretty soon an ambulance arrived to see to us. By that time I was feeling better, but I had lost track of Jody. Where was she? Had she disappeared? Gone home?

Had I lost my chance already?

Most of my aches were going away, but they were replaced by one in my heart. It couldn't be over so quickly. Could it? Before we had even had a chance to talk? I started looking around wildly, but I didn't see her. Maybe the cops would give me her information. Hadn't she said something about being a school teacher? I would go to every school in the city until I found her.

I had to do something. She was my denya. My mate. We hadn't gone through all of this trouble for me to lose her so quickly.

"Are you okay?"

I spun around at the sound of Jody's voice. She

had two steaming mugs in her hands and offered one to me. "Where did you go?" I asked as I took the mug, the answer evident in the warm drink.

"I thought we could use something like this. It's just cider, and it's not even spiked. But it'll be good." She took a sip and sat down on the bench. I quickly joined her.

She was right. The drink was good. Sweet with a hint of spice. It was nothing like what we had back home, but I was getting used to the tastes of Earth. "So is this a favorite drink?" I asked.

"I like it well enough," said Jody. Then she laughed. It was a bit frantic, as if she was just realizing everything that we had gone through. "I feel like I've been around you my entire life," she said. "Is that weird? It feels weird. Especially since you don't even know if I like apple cider."

Apple cider was irrelevant. I knew the important things. Things that went beyond the recognition of our mating bond. "I know you're brave. Strong. Resourceful. You faced off against that alien in ways that many people wouldn't have been able to handle. I'd like to know what your favorite drinks are. But I think I've seen hints of all the important stuff. Preferences for snacks and beverages will come in time."

"You seem certain of that," she said with a smile. "We might never see each other again after tonight."

"No, that's not happening." It probably wasn't the right thing to say. Too forceful. Too absolute. Most humans still didn't understand the denya bond. They didn't know how we could know that we were meant to be together. They didn't sense this thing the same way that we did. But luckily for me, Jody seemed into it.

"I'd ask you to dinner, but I'm kind of afraid to go to any other public place right now. Like there are other aliens just waiting to capture me. I think I just need to head home."

I didn't want our night to end. But I could feel exhaustion nipping at me as well. It had been a hell of a night. "I want to see you again."

She looked at me for several moments, and I thought she might offer me her communicator information. Then she placed her hand on my thigh. "Want to come back to my place?"

It was more than I could hope for. But we hadn't talked. I knew some Detyens would be happy to take her up on her offer without ever explaining what it could mean. But I wasn't one of them. Even though joining with her would save my life, she needed to know what it meant. I couldn't take that choice away from her.

But she did not seem to sense what I was thinking about. Her fingers curled in and I hoped they would leave a mark. "I don't sleep with guys on the first date anymore," she said. "But I'm pretty sure tonight counts for like ten dates. So we can figure out the rest of that later."

I could just kiss her. Could do everything before sealing the actual act. Then I could explain the importance. Both of us needed it. We had survived. It was time to celebrate.

"Lead the way."

I really didn't sleep with guys on the first date. Really. I promise.

But Aldyn was different. And that night was at least ten dates combined. Maybe a lifetime. Excitement sizzled within me as I led him back to my apartment. I was glad I had just cleaned. I could be messy at times. But the gods must've been smiling down on me that night. I wanted to kiss him. Wanted to reach out and hold his hand and tug him close.

But I was pretty sure if I started kissing him I wasn't going to stop. So we stayed separate on the short walk. Then I led him up the rickety stairs that led to the door to my apartment. It was small. Unimpressive. But it was all mine. And that was worth something. Once the door closed behind him, the place felt tiny.

Aldyn wasn't that big. But he was big enough to take up enough space that I couldn't forget he was here. And I was happy. We took off our coats and I hung them in the closet. Aldyn still looked kind of bruised, though it was difficult to tell between the markings he naturally had on his gold skin and what Evil Santa had done to him. I wanted to kiss him and make it all better.

But suddenly, I was exhausted. All of the night just crashed down over me and I realized what we had been through. How we had survived. Damn, that was crazy.

A good host would have offered Aldyn a drink. I just stumbled towards the couch and collapsed. He rushed over after me, maybe concerned for my well-being, maybe concerned that it suddenly looked like he wasn't going to get any.

"Are you alright?" he asked, his hand going to my shoulder as if that was enough to steady me.

"We survived. What the fuck? What *was* that?" An evil alien had held us hostage. What even was my life? And here I was with a different alien, hoping he could soothe away all of my fears, could make me forget for the night what had really happened.

The tears caught me by surprise. I didn't even know I was on the verge of crying until sobs wracked my body and I could barely breathe. Aldyn wrapped his arms around me and held me close. It felt nice. Nicer than I would have expected. And I didn't want it to end. Thankfully, the tears didn't last that long. But I knew I did not look very hot. I had always been an ugly crier. It's why I tried not to ever do it.

I had to get control of the situation. I had to make things better. I cupped Aldyn's cheek and leaned in close. But before I could kiss him, he grinned at me. "Where's your bedroom?" he asked.

That was more like it. Maybe we could get things moving along.

There wasn't really any mystery about where the bedroom was. It was only a one bedroom apartment. There was exactly one closed door. That was where the bedroom was. He laced our fingers together and tugged me up from the couch before leading me into the room. I let my body press against his and tried to imagine what it would feel like once our clothes came off. He sat me down on the bed and dropped to his knees.

Yes. This was looking up. But instead of putting his hands on me, he reached for my shoes and slipped them off before taking off his own.

Okay, he was practical. I could take that. I could take all of him.

"Lay down," he said.

"I think we're missing a couple steps." It might have been sexier and more flirtatious if a yawn had cut me off in the middle of saying it.

Aldyn just waited until I lay down. And then he got in right beside me. He put his arms around me and tucked me in close to him. It was nice. Nicer than I knew it could feel.

And in its own way, it was even scarier than anything that Evil Santa had tried to do to us. Not scary in a way that meant I was going to be injured, but scary in a way that I knew something was about to change. Something massive. It was at just the edge of my conscience to ask what, but before I could grab onto the thought, my eyes drifted closed and I found myself surrendering to sleep.

I didn't dream. Not any dreams that I could remember. Though there was half a thought about calamari. It dissolved into nothingness before I could grasp the memory. And when I woke, sunlight streamed in.

And I was alone.

Not the first time I had woken up alone in bed after inviting a man to join me. But I was shocked at how much it hurt. My stomach dropped and I ached. Why? Why had he left? Why did I care? Was I not good enough?

I had to stop thinking it. If I kept thinking about it, I was just going to go crazy. Guys always left. And besides, it wasn't like I really knew him. We had just been thrown together in a crazy situation and that was it. There was nothing more. I didn't even care about him. I didn't even know his last name.

Was Aldyn even his real name? No way to know.

I would move on. And it wasn't like we had even slept together. Well. We haven't had sex. So it was okay. I'd be fine.

Right?

I turned over and curled up into a ball, still burrowed under the covers as if the warmth and softness of my mattress and blanket were enough to shield me from the harsh reality of the world. No one stayed.

No one cared.

I wasn't worth it.

Was that bacon?

There were only a few things that could pull me

out of my pity party and the scent of cooking meat was one of them. I threw the covers off and got out of bed. I was still wearing the clothes from last night, everything except my shoes. The shoes that Aldyn had so carefully taken off.

And there he was, standing in my kitchen and taking two sandwiches out of a bag from a restaurant that was just down the street.

"I thought you must be hungry," he said. "I got two different sandwiches. So whichever one you like more you can have. The cashier didn't know if you had a favorite order or anything."

He'd gone and gotten me breakfast? I didn't know if a guy had ever done that for me before.

I marched right up to him and captured his lips' searing kiss. This was what we were supposed to do the night before. This was what we were supposed to do forever, a small part of me whispered. But my grumbling stomach interrupted what I was sure was going to be one hell of a make out session and I pulled back with a sheepish grin. "I guess I am hungry," I had to say. I realized I hadn't even eaten dinner the night before. Of course I was starving.

But Aldyn was smiling at me as he handed me a sandwich. Bacon and eggs and cheese and bread.

Was there a better combination? I had taken two bites when the smile dropped off his face. He put his sandwich down and looked at me seriously.

"We need to talk."

[14]

ALDYN

I had planned to wait.

What was another few minutes, an hour, when it came to the rest of my life? Our lives? But as I stood there in Jody's kitchen. I knew I couldn't wait another minute.

My body craved her. I didn't know how much longer I could resist. But she needed to know this before we went any further. She took another bite of her sandwich before putting it down, and then she took a seat at her small kitchen table.

I sat opposite her. I would have rather held her close as I spoke, but it was probably better than we weren't touching. I didn't know how she would react. There were horror stories of Detyens proclaiming that they'd found their mate and their mate rejecting them. Would she? I didn't know. I couldn't know. But she needed to know who she was to me. She needed to know what I wanted.

And I wanted everything.

"What's going on, Aldyn?" she asked.

I should've let her finish her sandwich. Especially now that the words were caught in my throat. We had survived the horrors that had been thrown at us the night before, so why did this seem harder than the actual battle we had engaged in? I didn't know. I couldn't know.

"Do you know much about Detyens?" I asked. Some humans were fascinated by us. They looked up every bit of information they could find. Especially a couple of years ago, when my people had helped rescue the planet from certain destruction. There was a growing Detyen population and more and more of my brethren were finding their mates each year. Did she know about that? Did she care? Or was she one of the humans who didn't pay much attention to the aliens who were coming to this planet?

"I remember seeing a few news reports," she said. "But I can't say that I dedicated too much time to my research. I was busy." She looked away from me as she said busy. I didn't know what it was supposed to mean, and I wasn't about press. Her life before we met was her life. I wanted to know everything she would tell me and more, but it didn't have to be today.

"There's a lot to tell," I said. I wasn't even sure where to start. The destruction of my planet? The fact that we died if we didn't find our mates? The Detyen Legion?

"How about you just start with what you're trying to say right now?" she asked.

Good idea. I looked up and met her eyes. There was no holding back anymore. "You're my mate."

She blinked several times and looked surprised. "Your... mate? What?"

It wasn't rejection. It wasn't a joyful acceptance either, but it was a start.

"Detyens recognize our mates, our denyai, when we see them. I recognized you from the moment I saw you. Clearly I didn't say anything since we were a little busy." I didn't know what I would have done if we hadn't been in the midst of the crisis. Asked her to get a drink with me? Pressed her against the wall and kissed her until she begged for more? Offered her my communicator information? The possibilities were endless.

"I guess we were busy," she agreed. "But I'm not

anybody's mate. I'm a human. Not a Detyen or whatever."

I could bring up news reports. I could bring up the profiles that I had read in magazines. A few mated couples had sort of become celebrities after it became known. But I didn't think that she was rejecting the concept of matehood. I was pretty sure this was more personal. "You are," I said. "And from everything I've seen so far you're amazing. Everything I could have wanted."

"But not someone you chose." She stood up from the table and turned around, pacing the length of the room and then coming back to rest her hands on the back of the chair. "Free will is important. You have to be able to choose who you want."

That wasn't the argument I'd expected. I didn't want to fight her. Didn't want to tell her that she was wrong. So I stood up and moved to put my arms around her. She didn't pull away from the touch. "You don't have to accept me right now." It hurt to say those words, but it was true. I had time. And I would never force her. "But I think you like me. And I know I like you. So why don't we give this a chance? See where things go? We can forget about the mating. But I didn't want to go any further without telling you."

Her thumb made circles against my arm, the sensation strangely erotic despite the situation. "I'm not saying no to mating. Or well, sex, I guess." She paused for several moments and then looked up at me. "Don't you die if you don't mate?"

It was my turn to look away. But she was right. We did. "I'm not yet thirty. There's no rush."

"So if we did then would you like own me, or immediately get me pregnant, or anything like that?" She didn't look happy about that.

"Of course not! I would never own you. You would be my equal. You *are* my equal. As for children? That is something we would need to discuss." Where did humans get ideas like that?

She seemed to be considering something. I didn't dare to hope. And then she grinned and hope bloomed in my heart.

"I guess it's nice to know that you're serious from the beginning. I say we give it a shot."

If I let myself think about it for too long, I was going to start doubting. And by too long I meant for more than ten seconds.

Aldyn had saved my life. He had fought off an evil alien who wanted to abscond with me. And he had bought me breakfast. That made him a better boyfriend than anyone I had dated so far. That probably said more about my dating history or the kind of guys I let pick me up than Aldyn's quality, but it was the best I could do.

I wanted him. He said I was his mate. What was the point in waiting?

Somehow in the middle of our discussion, his revelation, I had finished eating my sandwich. I shoved the wrapper aside and laced our fingers together. "Come on."

He was looking at me with an expression I couldn't quite describe. Awe came kind of close. But I didn't know how to deal with that. Awe was terrifying. And it was sure to wear off. But I wanted to grab onto this thing for as long as I could and hold it close. I felt sure of Aldyn, sure that there was something real between us. I just had to give myself over to it.

But I was also nervous in a way I had never been nervous before. This wasn't like the impersonal and barely satisfying encounters I had given up on years ago. This was the start of something real. Something that could last forever.

Aldyn tilted my chin up and our eyes met. He gave me a crooked smile that made my heart flip over. "We're not going to do anything you don't want to do," he said.

I wanted to do it all. And a small part of me just wanted to tug him back down onto the bed and cuddle for the rest of the day. But certain parts of my body were screaming at me to do more. To make a move. To demand that he get down on his knees and worship me.

Maybe we'd save that for round two.

The time for hesitation was over. I tugged my shirt off in one smooth motion and shimmied out of my pants. It didn't take much more to have me standing completely naked in front of Aldyn. His mouth dropped open, and this time I wasn't imagining it when I saw that his black eyes were red.

How was that possible?

I didn't really care.

Whatever tricks came from him being a Detyen, whatever quirks there were with him being an alien, we would figure that out later.

Right now I wanted to figure out something much more fundamental.

Compatibility.

Were we right together?

Yes. I didn't need him thrusting between my thighs for me to figure that out. But I wanted it. And I was done waiting.

"Take off your clothes," I told him. I didn't know what had him hesitating. Especially not with the bulge I could see straining against his pants.

Aldyn didn't need to be told twice. His lips found mine and it was like a dream. He set my body alight in ways I didn't know were possible. We tumbled back to the bed and he took control. I didn't like giving it up. Especially today. Especially now. But it was different with him. He made me feel safe. He had already proved that he was going to stay. And so I let myself surrender to it.

When his fingers found the heat of my core, I let out a gasp and spread my legs even further. And when his lips followed quickly, I couldn't stop the curses that I let out even if I had tried. Not that I wanted him to stop. I never wanted him to stop.

He needed to keep going. To do more.

And he did. It was wickedness. Wantonness. And I wanted more.

It didn't take much for me to start gasping, breaths labored as my body rippled around him. And still he had not planted himself inside me. I needed to feel all of him. To feel joined in that most fundamental way.

I looked down at him and those eyes of his were still red when he saw me. He slowly kissed his way up my body, and I could feel the tension in his, his unfulfilled arousal. "We can wait," he promised, his voice raspy with want.

"Make me wait another minute and I'll do... something." I could barely think past the pleasure and Aldyn didn't need to be told twice.

And then it was even better. Our bodies joined, moving in unison. This kind of connection should not have been possible, not between the two of us. We came from different ends of the galaxy. Different species. But somehow it was more right than ever. And as he emptied himself into me I could feel some sort of awareness snap into place.

The bond he had talked about. I might not have recognized him from the first. But I knew it now. My mate.

It was like there was a cord embedded right under my heart and I could almost see it, could feel it reaching out to Aldyn. Was it real? A physical connection that I couldn't quite see? Metaphysical? Weird alien bullshit?

At the moment I couldn't care. I was drunk on pleasure and just wanted more.

We lay together, limbs casually entangled, and in that moment I was very happy that I had been held hostage by Evil Alien Santa.

It had brought me close to Aldyn. Had brought me this impossible thing that was blooming between us. This thing that was going to grow stronger every day.

It wasn't love. Not yet. But even after just a day together, I could feel the embers beginning to ignite. One day. Probably sooner than I'd be ready to admit.

But I couldn't stop smiling. For the first time in my life, I was ready.

And my body was hungry for him.

I looked over at Aldyn with a grin. "Want to go again?"

He smiled and kissed me.

One Year Later

Every year.

I did this every freaking year. Three days before Christmas and I still had a ton of gifts buy. What was I thinking?

At least this year I wasn't doing it alone.

"Do you have your defense spray?" Aldyn asked.

I tapped my front pocket where the small canister fit snugly. "Yup. Do you have the anti-security measures?" I asked.

He held up a small tablet. It was supposed to be able to disengage force fields. It wasn't exactly legal. But it wasn't illegal either. And given our experience, I wasn't taking another chance.

"Knife? he asked.

"Oh yeah."

"Shopping list?" I asked.

"All of the teachers are on a list. Plus the gifts you're giving for your class. We can do this. No getting held hostage this year."

"No getting held hostage," I agreed. I leaned in and gave him a kiss. We laced our fingers together and headed for the entrance of the store.

It had been quite the year. From our first night together followed by that magnificent first day together. And every day since then. It wasn't that we never fought, or never disagreed. It wasn't perfect.

But it was pretty damn close.

I had never been so happy in my life. I didn't know if I could be happier.

Aldyn and I fit like I had never known I could fit with another person. I no longer was wondering what could be. What kind of relationship I might one day be able to fool someone into embarking on with me.

Now I had a guy who saw me for who I was. Who wanted me for who I was. Who loved me for who I was.

Yes, sometimes he left his towels on the bathroom floor. And sometimes he didn't fill up the dishwasher. But those were just minor issues. Something ultimately I didn't care about too much. The dishes got cleaned eventually.

I didn't know why we were heading back into the same store after everything that had happened last year. Maybe it was foolish. Maybe we were being nostalgic.

What we weren't was taking any chances.

There had been an investigation into how Evil Santa had held us hostage and the technology he had used. But the police hadn't managed to find out much. I guess that was what happened when your captor got sucked into a tentacle dimension.

The portal device was a piece of technology that we didn't have on Earth. I didn't know whose hands it ended up in.

I hope it didn't get used for evil.

But most days we didn't think about Evil Santa.

We went on with our lives. We figured out who we were together and what we wanted from the future.

And it was good.

And this holiday season, I was happy to be celebrating our first anniversary. The first of many to come.

"I love you," I told Aldyn with a kiss.

He smiled as we pulled apart and then kissed my forehead. "You are my denya."

Did you like this story?
Please consider leaving a review at your favorite retailer.
And if you *really* liked this story, share it with a friend!

What to read next:
The Alien Reindeer's Wild Ride
She'll be home for Christmas... even if she has to steal a ship to get there!

She'll be home for Christmas... even if she has to steal a ship to get there!

Rowan has missed out on the last three big family holidays, and she's determined not to miss another. Holiday travel is always a mess, and even worse when she needs to get from Mars to Minnesota. Every flight is booked through the New Year and things aren't looking good. Until someone whispers the name *Dashiel Blitz* and gives her a bit of holiday hope.

He just wants to spread good cheer...

Dash makes a life shepherding sick children from planet to planet so they can be with their parents or get medical treatment. Rowan isn't like his usual passengers, but his soul sings when they meet and he can't say no. She's on his ship for a ride, but he wants even more.

One tiny problem...

Dash isn't just a pilot. He's a reindeer shifter and he needs to keep that a secret if he wants to stay safe. But if Rowan is his mate she needs to know the truth. And when a delay in their trip threatens to strand her on the wrong side of Earth, he may have to reveal himself in the most dramatic way possible.

Could a determined human woman want an alien shifter for a mate? Or will their wild ride end with a crash and burn?

Keep reading for a peek at the first chapter!

Looking for something else? Kate Rudolph has a heart pounding collection or paranormal and sci-fi romance stories for you! Bundles, bears, audiobooks, aliens, and more. Check out your options in the list below. You can find out all you need to know at www.katerudolph.net.

Detyen Warriors

Detya was destroyed a hundred years ago. These doomed warriors are out to find justice... and their mates.

The Detyen Warriors series brings you kick butt heroines, alpha alien heroes, fated mates, and relationships strong enough to span the galaxy!

The entire series is also available in audio!

Soulless

Ruthless

Heartless

Faultless

Endless

Zulir Warrior Mates

Kidnapped humans. Alien Warriors. Electric wings.

The Zulir Warrior Mates series brings you human heroines and heroes abducted from Earth who find love – and wings! – with the alien warriors who rescue them. *Also available in audio!*

Synnr's Saint

Synnr's Hope

Synnr's Spark

Alien Holiday Romance

Christmas… in space????

These alien holiday romances look beyond Earth's winter holidays and ring in the season across the galaxy! *Select titles available in audio.*

Snowed in with the Alien Beast

The Alien's Winter Gift

The Alien Reindeer's Wild Ride

Trapped with her Alien Mate

Alien Outlaws

Outlaws, schemes, and love... it's all there in the Alien Outlaws series...

Andie Munster is sick of life on Ixilta, the planet she got dumped on after being abducted from Earth six years ago. And when the mysterious and dangerous Xandr shows up looking for a way off the planet, she's half-prisoner, half-co-conspirator in a wild rush to escape.

Rogue Alien's Escape

Rogue Alien's Woman

Rogue Alien's Secret

Rogue Alien's Legacy

Mated to the Alien

Fated Mate Alien Romance

Detyens are doomed to die young if they don't find their fated mates.

Follow along as these mated pairs fight off aliens, corrupt dictators, prejudiced humans, pirates, and more! The books can be read or listened to in any order, though some characters show up in multiple stories.

Select books available in audio.

Pick a book and jump into the action today!

Ruwen

Tyral

Stoan

Cyborg

Krayter

Kayleb

Shayn

Braxtyn

Doryan

Stealing the Alpha

The thief takes what she wants, but the alpha keeps what's his...

Join shifter thief Mel as she clashes with lion alpha Luke in an explosive trilogy of two opposites who can't keep away from one another.

Also available in audio!

The Alpha Heist

Entangled with the Thief

In the Alpha's Bed

Find more by Kate Rudolph at www.katerudolph.net

Kate Rudolph is science fiction romance author who lives in Indiana. She loves writing about kick butt heroines and the steamy heroes who love them. She's been devouring romance novels since she was too young to be reading them and had to hide her books so no one would take them away. She couldn't imagine a better job in this world than writing romances and sharing them with her fellow readers.

If you enjoyed this story, please consider leaving a review.

Keep up to date with what's coming soon, get access to exclusive giveaways, and hang out with Kate online in her Facebook group! Kate Rudolph's Detyen Dreamers is where Kate Rudolph fans can hang out and talk about the latest in alien romance.

READY TO BECOME A SUPERFAN?

Patreon is a community of readers where you can interact directly with Kate Rudolph and be the first one to get access to her books... weeks and months before they are published!

What else do patrons get?

- Read books chapter by chapter as they are written
- Exclusive discounts to Kate's website
- A free book of the month
- And more!

Check out Patreon at www.patreon.com/katerudolph.

WHAT TO READ NEXT: THE ALIEN REINDEER'S
WILD RIDE

Rowan Lambert rushed from her final meeting of the day and dodged around a droid cart, trying to make it to the ticketing station as quickly as she could. She was supposed to be getting on a shuttle and heading back to Earth, but a last minute appointment had sent her scrambling to reschedule. And an oversight—on the part of the shuttle company, definitely not her fault—meant she didn't have a ticket to replace the one she'd given up.

Normally it wouldn't be a problem. There were dozens of shuttles that flew passengers between Earth and Mars every week, but this was no normal week. Seven days until the big holiday, and every seat was taken on every major and minor vessel leaving the planet.

But that didn't stop Ro from running. She'd heard a rumor from a trustworthy source that a batch of tickets was about to open up. Thirty lucky people would get seats, but they were bound to sell out in minutes. And the only way to get one of the seats was to show up in person and purchase it at the ticket counter. Barbaric, but it was the only flight home and she needed to be on it.

Was it still home if she hadn't set foot in the place in more than three years? Four? Damn, how long had she been away?

Ro wasn't going to think about that now. Her sister would give her enough grief when she learned about the ticket mix up. No need to borrow trouble by thinking about her own failings.

She was going to make it home this time. She didn't let herself think about how she'd been sure of that last year, too. It wasn't her fault that her company's biggest client had shown up unrequested to speak to her about a large sale. Was she just supposed to let millions of credits slip through her fingers? The year before a giant storm had stopped all traffic between the planets, and before that, Ro had figured missing one holiday wouldn't matter too much. She wasn't going to miss the fourth in a row. She hadn't seen her nephew since he was barely more than six and now that he was edging on ten, she didn't even know if he'd remember her.

No. She was going to make it.

But the line at the ticket counter was disheartening. There were at least fifty people, humans and all kinds of aliens, crowded in front of the one open window and clearly ready to pay an exorbitant amount if it meant getting off Mars in time.

If there were only thirty tickets there was no way she'd get one, not with this many people around. And it would take a miracle to get them to leave.

A miracle or a bit of… creativity.

She felt a twinge of guilt as she pulled out her communicator, but she didn't let it stop her from putting it up to her ear and speaking in an exaggerated whisper. "Tickets at the south station? You're sure?" The person standing in front of her whipped their head around and Ro looked down, as if she didn't want to give away the secret. "A hundred credits? You've got to be joking." The tickets they were all in line for were five times that price. "I'm waiting for someone. Do you think they'll still be there in half an hour?" The person in front of her leaned close, trying to hear without being obvious, and Ro spoke just a little louder, making sure they didn't miss out.

"Okay, I'll head over when he gets there. Save us a spot."

She stuck her communicator back in her pocket and pretended to look for the companion she'd just made up.

Whispers swirled around, and after a minute, two people around her broke away and took off for the fabled tickets at the south station. Another handful followed soon after. That still left a few dozen people waiting for tickets here, but it gave Ro a fighting shot.

And it wasn't her fault if people were gullible enough to place their faith in a stranger's whispered comm conversation.

It took another half hour before she made it to the window, and she could tell by the apologetic look on the attendant's face what she was going to say. "I'm sorry, the block of tickets has sold out. The next open shuttle is in eight days. Or we have flights available out of the solar system right now."

Ro grit her teeth. "Is there *anything* before that? What about a flight to the moon? I can get a connection there."

The ticket woman grimaced. "All inner solar system shuttles are booked, I'm afraid."

"I *need* to get home, I've been gone too long. I

can't let..." Ro bit off the rest of that sentence. The same was true for everyone who'd tried to buy tickets, and it wasn't like complaining would make any appear out of thin air.

The ticket woman gave the still gathered people a furtive glance before lowering her voice. "Dash might be able to help. Dashiel Blitz. But keep it quiet. I'm sorry."

What kind of name was Dashiel Blitz?

Ro let it roll around in her mind as she backed away from the ticket counter and weaved through the soon to be disappointed crowd. She'd never heard of the guy before, but if he could help he had to have a ship or access to one. The *shuttles* were all booked, but private vessels had to have space. Hopefully.

Wherever he was, she needed to find him before the woman at the ticket counter gave out his name to more people. She had credits to offer, but who knew how much space he had. If there was enough room on his ship for an extra passenger, she had to make sure it was her.

She was getting to Earth, even if she had to bribe a captain to do it.

ARE YOU A STARR HUNTRESS?

Do you love to read sci fi romance about strong, independent women and the sexy alien males who love them?

Starr Huntress is a coalition of the brightest Starrs in romance banding together to explore uncharted territories.

If you like your men horny- maybe literally- and you're equal opportunity skin color-because who doesn't love a guy with blue or green skin?- then join us as we dive into swashbuckling space adventure, timeless romance, and lush alien landscapes.

Newsletter sign up: http://eepurl.com/b_NJyr

More from Starr Huntress authors at www. starrhuntress.com

www.ingramcontent.com/pod-product-compliance
Lightning Source LLC
Chambersburg PA
CBHW032039180726

48284CB00008B/2656